The JOURNEY of the NOBLE GNARBLE

by DANIEL ERRICO

illustrations by TIFFANY TURRILL

EMERALD
BOOK CO.

Published by Emerald Book Company
Austin, TX
www.emeraldbookcompany.com

Distributed by Emerald Book Company

For ordering information or special discounts for bulk purchases, please contact Emerald Book Company at PO Box 91869, Austin, TX 78709, 512.891.6100.

Design and composition by Greenleaf Book Group LLC
Cover design by Greenleaf Book Group LLC
Illustrations by Tiffany Turrill

Publisher's Cataloging-In-Publication Data
(Prepared by The Donohue Group, Inc.)
Errico, Daniel J.
   The journey of the Noble Gnarble / by Daniel J. Errico ; illustrated by Tiffany Turrill. -- 1st ed.
      p. : col. ill. ; cm.
   Summary: Far below the ocean waves, a gnarble left his cozy bed along the ocean floor and headed to the surface for a glimpse of sun and sky. Though he can't swim far with little fins and floppy tails, his mind would not be changed by fish who tried to make him to stay. Did he quit when he discovered all the creatures in his way?
   Interest age group: 003-006.
   ISBN: 978-1-934572-89-4
   1. Fishes--Juvenile fiction. 2. Animals, Mythical--Juvenile fiction. 3. Persistence--Juvenile fiction. 4. Fishes--Fiction. 5. Imaginary creatures--Fiction. 6. Persistence--Fiction. 7. Sea stories. I. Turrill, Tiffany. II. Title.
PZ7.E77 Jou 2011
[E]   2011927561

Part of the Tree Neutral® program, which offsets the number of trees consumed in the production and printing of this book by taking proactive steps, such as planting trees in direct proportion to the number of trees used: www.treeneutral.com

TreeNeutral®

Manufactured by iPrinting on acid-free paper
Manufactured in Shanghai, China in August, 2011
Batch No. 1

11 12 13 14 15 16   10 9 8 7 6 5 4 3 2 1

First Edition

TO THE EXPLORER

Far below the ocean waves,
a gnarble lay in bed.

All night long his gnarble dreams
kept swimming in his head.

He dreamt a dream of swimming
up to see the sky above,

Lit up by the sun in colors
he just knew he'd love.

But gnarbles never swam that high,
    their fins were much too small.

Their tails were thin and floppy,
    which didn't help at all.

This gnarble liked his fins
    and had no problem with his tail.

So when he woke, he knew that
    he just couldn't, wouldn't fail.

"I'm swimming up above the waves
to see the sky of blue.

I've never seen it even once,
and now it's time I do."

The other gnarbles warned him
that he shouldn't swim so high,

As did the blyfish family that
always swam close by.

"No gnarble's ever swum that high,
it simply isn't done.

A blyfish might just make the trip,
but we know you're not one."

"Gnarbles don't have flappers
like all us blyfish do.

You don't even have koggers
like the swimming gungaloo."

But the gnarble didn't listen,
and he left his friends behind.

No silly blyfish family
could ever change his mind.

He swam up past the boulders
made of spongy gishy-gosh,

And flew right by the herd
of floating, feeding fipple-fosh.

His fins were getting tired,
 but he knew he couldn't stop.

So he kept swimming faster,
 trying hard to reach the top.

Just then a hungry warckel
   blocked the gnarble with his fin.

He grabbed him by his tail and
   brought him right up to his chin.

"I've never had a gnarble,
   this would be a tasty treat.

But you're much too thin and bony
   for a fish like me to eat."

So the gnarble just kept swimming,
and didn't dare to stop,

Until he heard the sound
of a great big bubble POP!

He turned around to see
that he was in a bit of trouble.

The sound he heard was that
of a silver subbalubble.

The gnarble tried to hide somewhere
that he could safely stay,

But the subbalubble saw him
and was headed right his way.

"Oh Mister Subbalubble,
    please don't eat me up for lunch.

I'll bring a yummy plant instead,
    for you to sit and munch."

"I've never seen a gnarble
    try to swim this high before.

What is it, little fishy, that
    you're up here looking for?"

"If I could see the sky just once,
    I'd be a happy fish.

To do one flip above the waves
    would be my only wish."

"Well sorry, silly gnarble,
but I cannot let you go.

It's subbalubble dinner time
—you should've stayed below."

The gnarble cowered back in fear
and shook from fin to fin,

But then he saw a school of fish
called shiny glimmy glin.

The glimmy glin swam right past
the subbalubble's face,

And the gnarble grabbed a glimmy fin
and quickly left that place.

The gnarble swam up higher still,
    until he saw some light.

He knew it had to be the sun and,
    Oh, was it a sight!

Closely by, a plink was sleeping,
    lying on his back.

He rubbed his giant belly
    as he dreamed about a snack.

The gnarble smiled happily
and set his fins a swimming.

He didn't see the plink wake up,
for he was busy grinning.

The gnarble almost made it
to the surface of the sea,

But the plink chomped down and
swallowed him as if he were a pea.

The gnarble sat inside the plink
and started softly crying.

He'd never make it out,
so was there any point in trying?

The gnarble knew he'd come too close
to quit and give up now.

"There must be someway out of here.
There's got to be, somehow."

So the gnarble swam around inside,
trying very hard to think.

And while he did, his floppy tail
was tickling the plink.

The plink was very ticklish,
and he couldn't hold it in.

He tried to cover up his laugh
with his giant plinkish fin.

His mouth was open long enough
for the gnarble to swim free.

He swam so fast, the hungry plink
did not have time to see.

Far above the ocean floor,
  above the gnarbles' homes,

Above the blyfish families
  and dancing water-gnomes,

Above the swimming gungaloo
and slimy dundledun,

A gnarble flipped above the waves
and smiled at the sun!